# Improving
# Comprehension

r ages 7–8

# Contents

# Introduction

*Improving Comprehension* includes a range of interesting and exciting texts for sharing with pupils and using for reading comprehension. The texts have been carefully selected to be appropriate to the age group and to cover a range of text types. They reflect the demands of the Primary Framework for Literacy and in particular they following the learning objectives for Year 3. The accompanying comprehension worksheets are differentiated at three levels and are designed to be used by individuals or small groups. *Notes for teachers* are provided at the bottom of each worksheet providing guidance on how to get the most from the texts and how to approach the questions on the sheet.

For monitoring and recording purposes an *Individual record sheet* is provided on page 4 detailing reading and writing levels appropriate for Year 3. You may also find it helpful to refer to the *Contents* page where the 'texts' are linked to the relevant Assessment Focuses.

## How to use the book and CD-ROM together

The book has fifteen 'texts', which can be projected on to a whiteboard for whole class use using the CD-ROM, or photocopied/printed for use with small groups or individuals. Sharing the text either on screen or on paper provides lots of opportunities for speaking and listening, for decoding words through a phonic approach, for reading and re-reading for meaning and for satisfaction and enjoyment in shared success.

For each text there are three comprehension worksheets at different ability levels to enable teachers to differentiate across the ability range. An animal picture at the top of the sheet indicates the level of the worksheet. The 'cat' exercises are at the simplest level; the 'dog' exercises are at the next level; the 'rabbit' exercises are at the most advanced level. You may decide to give some pupils the 'cat' worksheet and then decide, on the basis of their success, to ask them to complete the 'dog' worksheet. A similar approach could be taken with the 'dog' and 'rabbit' sheets.

After reading the text with the pupils the teacher should discuss the tasks with the children, ensuring that they understand clearly how to complete the worksheet and reminding them to answer the questions using full sentences and correct punctuation.

## National Curriculum levels

The worksheets are aimed at the following ability levels:

*Cat* worksheets are for pupils working towards Level 2.
*Dog* worksheets are for pupils working at Level 2.
*Rabbit* worksheets are for pupils who are working confidently at Level 2 and are progressing towards Level 3.

# Individual record sheet

**Pupil's name:** _____

**Date of birth:** _____

## Reading Level 2

☐ I can show understanding when reading simple texts.
☐ My reading of simple texts is generally accurate.
☐ I can express opinions about major events or ideas in stories, poems and non-fiction.
☐ I can use phonic skills in reading unfamiliar words and establishing meaning.
☐ I can use graphic skills in reading unfamiliar words and establishing meaning.
☐ I can use syntactic skills in reading unfamiliar words and establishing meaning.
☐ I can use contextual skills in reading unfamiliar words and establishing meaning.

## Reading Level 3

☐ I can read a range of texts fluently and accurately.
☐ I can read independently.
☐ I use strategies appropriately to establish meaning.
☐ In my responses to fiction I show understanding of the main points and I express preferences.
☐ In my responses to non-fiction I show understanding of the main points and I express preferences.
☐ I know the order of the alphabet.
☐ I use my knowledge of the alphabet to locate books and find information.

## Writing Level 2

☐ My narrative writing communicates meaning.
☐ My non-narrative writing communicates meaning.
☐ I use appropriate and interesting vocabulary.
☐ I show some awareness of the reader.
☐ I can write a sequence of sentences to show ideas developing.
☐ My sentences are sometimes demarcated by capital letters and full stops.
☐ Usually, I can spell simple, monosyllabic words correctly or spell a phonetically plausible alternative.
☐ My letters are accurately formed.
☐ My letters are consistent in size.

## Writing Level 3

☐ My writing is often organised, imaginative and clear.
☐ I use the main features of different forms of writing.
☐ I am beginning to adapt my writing to different readers.
☐ I use sequences of sentences to extend ideas logically.
☐ I choose words for variety and interest.
☐ The basic grammatical structure of my sentences is usually correct.
☐ My spelling is usually accurate, including that of common, polysyllabic words.
☐ I use punctuation accurately to mark sentences, including full stops, capital letters and question marks.
☐ My handwriting is joined and legible.

# Fun at cub camp

This was the moment Jasmine had been waiting for. Her knees were shaking and her hands were sweaty. There was a nervous feeling inside her. It didn't feel like butterflies in her stomach, it felt more like caterpillars crawling around!

"Your turn Jasmine," said Akela.

This was it. Her brother had told her about it. The other cubs had told her about it.

"You'll never be able to do it, Jasmine," they had said.

Right, thought Jasmine, I'm going to do it.

"OK, are you ready?" asked Akela.

Jasmine nodded then rubbed her hands together to try to get the sweat off. She reached out for the rope and held it tightly. Before she had time to hesitate, the rope started to swing across Devil's Drop.

Jasmine looked down. No wonder it was called Devil's Drop! She held on even tighter and within seconds reached the other side. Baloo grabbed her and pulled her on to the safety of the platform. The rope went swinging back for the next person.

That wasn't that hard, thought Jasmine.

"Just wait till I tell Josh," she said to Baloo.

Andrew Brodie: Improving Comprehension for ages 7-8 © A&C Black Publishers Ltd 2008

## Fun at cub camp

Name: _____

Date: _____

**Write a full sentence for each answer. Don't forget to start each sentence with a capital letter and to end it with a full stop.**

1. How did Jasmine feel at the start of the story?

   _____

   _____

2. What did Jasmine have to do?

   _____

   _____

   _____

3. What was the name of the place that Jasmine had to cross?

   _____

   _____

4. Who was with Jasmine before she crossed the gap on the rope swing?

   _____

   _____

5. Who caught Jasmine on the other side of the gap?

   _____

   _____

**Notes for teachers**
Read the passage through to the children helping them to understand the story. They need to be aware that Jasmine is a girl member of cubs and that Akela and Baloo are cub leaders. Discuss the story with them to ensure that they understand that Jasmine is going on a big rope swing across a deep dip in the ground. If you feel that they are able to do so, help them to read the story themselves using their phonic skills to decode unfamiliar words.

Andrew Brodie: Improving Comprehension for ages 7-8 © A&C Black Publishers Ltd 2008

## Fun at cub camp

Name: _____

Date: _____

### Write a full sentence for each answer.

1. How do we know that Jasmine was nervous?

   _____

   _____

2. Who had told Jasmine that she would not be able to cross Devil's Drop on the rope swing?

   _____

   _____

3. Why did Jasmine rub her hands together?

   _____

   _____

4. How long was Jasmine on the rope swing for?

   _____

   _____

5. Who do you think Josh is?

   _____

   _____

6. Would you like to go on this rope swing?

   _____

   _____

**Notes for teachers**
Discuss the story with the children and make sure they realise that Jasmine is a girl scout who is about to swing on a big rope across a deep dip in the ground. They also need to be aware that Jasmine is a girl member of cubs and that Akela and Baloo are cub leaders. When answering question 5, point out that Jasmine refers to her brother earlier on in the story and that he could well be called 'Josh'.

7

## Fun at cub camp

### Answer the questions using a full sentence each time.

1.  List the three sensations that Jasmine felt because she was nervous.

    _____

    _____

    _____

2.  Why was Jasmine determined to cross the gap?

    _____

    _____

3.  Why did Jasmine hold the rope 'even tighter'?

    _____

    _____

4.  How did Jasmine feel after she had crossed the gap?

    _____

    _____

5.  Describe a time when you have felt nervous. What were you nervous about? Were you brave? What happened in the end?

    _____

    _____

    _____

**Notes for teachers**

Discuss the story with the children to ensure that they understand what Jasmine is about to do and how the author sets the scene and conveys Jasmine's feelings of anxiety. Help them to compose answers orally before writing anything down. They may need extra paper for the last task.

Andrew Brodie: Improving Comprehension for ages 7-8 © A&C Black Publishers Ltd 2008

# Amazing Alphabet

**A** is an animal with a

**B**ee upon its back.

**C** is a car that

**D**rives around a track.

**E** is an elephant

**F**lying through the air.

**G** is a giggling girl,

**H**ead of curly hair.

**I** is an ink blot

**J**ust spreading out so far.

**K** is a silly king

**L**icking out a jar.

**M**, a metal monster

**N**eeding batteries, new.

**O** is an octopus

**P**laying with his stew.

**Q** is quickly running,

and…

**R**eady for a rest.

**S** is a student learning

**T**ables for a test.

**U** is an umbrella,

**V**ery useful in the rain.

**W**, a whale with a

**X**ylophone on a train.

**Y** is a yellow yak being

**Z**ipped off to the vet.

All twenty-six letters in

The amazing alphabet.

Andrew Brodie: Improving Comprehension for ages 7-8 © A&C Black Publishers Ltd 2008

## Amazing Alphabet

Name: _____

Date: _____

**Ring the correct answers.**

1.  What is on the animal's back?

    banana        bee        boy        beast

2.  What is the king licking?

    a car        a battery        a jar        a train

3.  Who was learning tables for a test?

    a student        an octopus        a xylophone        a bee

**Answer the questions by completing the sentences.**

4.  What is the elephant doing?

    The elephant is _____.

5.  What colour is the yak?

    The yak is _____.

**Write a sentence to answer this question.**

6.  Where is the yak going?

    _____

    _____

    _____

**Notes for teachers**

Read the poem through with the children helping them to follow the order of the alphabet and talking about the words that rhyme. Help the children to compose a sentence to answer the final question, encouraging them to say the sentence out loud before writing it down. They might like to embellish the sentence by suggesting why the yak might be going to the vet!

Andrew Brodie: Improving Comprehension for ages 7-8 © A&C Black Publishers Ltd 2008

## Amazing Alphabet

Name: _____

Date: _____

**Ring the correct answers.**

1. What does the poem say is useful in the rain?

   ambulance          umbrella          student          alphabet

2. Which word in the poem is used to rhyme with 'new'?

   flu          queue          stew          crew

**Complete the sentences to answer the questions.**

3. How many letters are in the alphabet?

   There are _____ in the alphabet.

4. How many lines are there in the poem?

   There are _____ lines in the poem.

**Write sentences to answer these questions.**

5. Who has a head of curly hair?

   _____

   _____

6. What does the metal monster need?

   _____

   _____

**Notes for teachers**

Read the poem through with the children helping them to follow the order of the alphabet and looking at the rhyming words. Help them to compose sentences orally to answer the final two questions, before writing anything down.

Andrew Brodie: Improving Comprehension for ages 7-8 © A&C Black Publishers Ltd 2008

## Amazing Alphabet

Name: _____

Date: _____

1. Ring the word nearest in meaning to amazing.

long          wonderful          ridiculous          rhyming

**Write complete sentences to answer these questions.**

2. Where can the bee be found?

_____

_____

3. What is happening to the ink blot?

_____

_____

4. What does the word 'zipped' mean in the poem?

_____

_____

5. Explain how you can tell that the 'Amazing Alphabet' is a poem.

_____

_____

_____

6. Illustrate these lines from the poem on a separate sheet of paper: 'M, a metal monster...'

### Notes for teachers

Read the poem through with the children helping them to follow the order of the alphabet. Two children could take it in turns to read a line each, seeing if they can keep the rhythm going between them. The answer to question 4 should indicate an understanding that 'zipped' is used to mean 'taken quickly'. The features of a poem that pupils should recognise are the layout (all the lines are short and they start with capital letters) and the rhyming words.

Andrew Brodie: Improving Comprehension for ages 7-8 © A&C Black Publishers Ltd 2008

# Trees

There are millions of trees growing in this country.

Some trees lose their leaves in the autumn and grow new ones in the spring. These trees are called deciduous trees.

The leaves on a deciduous tree change colour in the autumn. Some of them turn brown, some turn yellow, some turn orange and some turn red. When the wind blows, the leaves fall off the branches and land on the ground.

This is why autumn is sometimes called 'the fall'. Often the dead leaves will become very dry and will rustle and scrunch when you walk through them.

Through the cold winter months the deciduous trees have no leaves and you can see all the branches and twigs very clearly.

In the spring, new leaves grow on the trees. They are fresh and bright green. All through the summer the trees are covered in beautiful green leaves.

Trees that don't lose their leaves in the winter are called evergreen trees because they are *ever green*. Evergreen trees include holly trees, pine trees and monkey puzzle trees.

Andrew Brodie: Improving Comprehension for ages 7-8 © A&C Black Publishers Ltd 2008

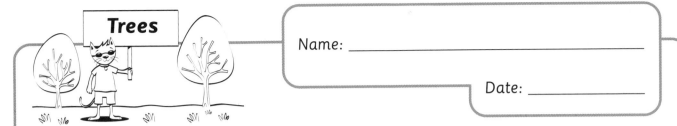

**Trees**

Name: _____

Date: _____

## Write a full sentence for each answer.

1.  What is the special name for trees that lose their leaves in the autumn?

    _____

    _____

2.  What is autumn sometimes called?

    _____

    _____

3.  What colours do the leaves turn in the autumn?

    _____

    _____

4.  When do the new leaves appear on the trees?

    _____

    _____

5.  What season is it now, autumn, winter, spring or summer?

    _____

    _____

6.  What will the next season be?

    _____

    _____

**Notes for teachers**
Read the passage through to the children helping them to understand it. If you feel that they are able to do so, help them to read it themselves using their phonic skills to decode unfamiliar words. Give them particular help with the word 'deciduous', encouraging them to separate it into syllables.

14

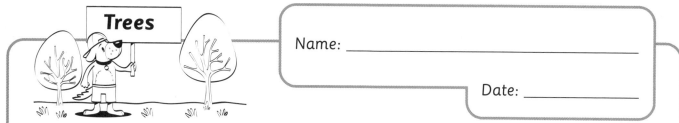

**Trees**

Name: _____

Date: _____

## Answer the questions about trees, using full sentences.

1. What is the special name for trees that lose their leaves in the autumn?

   _____

   _____

2. What is the special name for trees that don't lose their leaves in the autumn?

   _____

   _____

3. What helps the leaves to fall off the trees?

   _____

   _____

4. What season is it now?

   _____

   _____

5. Name some evergreen trees.

   _____

   _____

6. Can you see a tree out of the window? On a separate sheet of paper write some sentences to describe what it looks like. Think about how tall it is. How many branches does it have? How wide is its trunk? Does it have any leaves?

**Notes for teachers**

Read the passage through with the children helping them to understand the main points. Give them particular help with the word 'deciduous', encouraging them to separate it into syllables. Help them to develop their ideas orally for the last question before they write anything down.

Andrew Brodie: Improving Comprehension for ages 7-8 © A&C Black Publishers Ltd 2008

**Trees**

Name: _____

Date: _____

## Answer the questions about trees, using *full sentences*.

1.  Why do autumn leaves rustle when you walk through them?

    _____

    _____

2.  Why can you see the branches of deciduous trees so clearly in the winter?

    _____

    _____

3.  What do deciduous trees look like in summer?

    _____

    _____

4.  What month and what season is it now?

    _____

    _____

5.  Name some deciduous trees. You may need to look in the library or on the computer to find some ideas. Think about the shapes of the leaves that you often see on the ground.

    _____

    _____

    _____

    _____

**Notes for teachers**
Read the passage through with the children checking that they understand the main points. Give them particular help with the word 'deciduous', encouraging them to separate it into syllables. Discuss the current month and season. Can the children name all the months of the year in order and can they identify which months are in each season?

# Pete's surprise

Pete's birthday was coming up soon. This year his birthday was going to be during the half term holiday. He wanted a party but Mum and Dad said that parties were very expensive and they didn't think they could manage it this year.

Instead Pete invited his best friend Josh for tea, but Josh had made plans to go out that day. Oh well, perhaps he wouldn't be seeing his friends on his birthday but his grandparents were bound to come and see him, Pete thought to himself.

At last it was the day Pete had been waiting for, 23rd February, his eighth birthday. After bolting down his breakfast he got dressed and, waited impatiently for the postman to arrive. There were three birthday cards, and a present from his aunt.

Pete put the cards on the windowsill and started to do the new jigsaw that his aunt had given him. It was a map of the world with some pieces shaped like the creatures that lived in that part of the world. There were lion and zebra shapes in Africa, penguin shapes in the Antarctic and polar bears in the Arctic. It was fascinating and he spent most of the morning piecing it together.

After lunch, Pete realised that he was having a very quiet birthday and thought that perhaps it would have been better to be at school after all. In the middle of the afternoon his grandparents arrived with cards, presents and big hugs! A little later the doorbell went and in came Josh. Then the doorbell went again and two more of his friends arrived.

Pete was lost for words. What was happening? Within ten minutes twelve of his friends had arrived, as had three of his aunts and four cousins. It slowly dawned on Pete that it was a surprise party! Mum had made party food, Grandad had organised games and Gran had made a cake in the shape of a racing track.

As Pete lay in bed that night he felt that the surprise party had made his eighth birthday the best birthday ever!

Andrew Brodie: Improving Comprehension for ages 7-8 © A&C Black Publishers Ltd 2008

## Pete's surprise

Name: _____

Date: _____

**Ring the correct answers.**

1. Why did Mum and Dad say that Pete couldn't have a party?

   They were          It was too          It would          There was
   too busy.          cold.          be too          not enough
                                      expensive.          food.

2. Who arrived with 'big hugs'?

   his grandparents          his aunt          his mum          his
                                                                friends

3. How old was Pete on his birthday?

   six          seven          eight          nine

**Write the correct word to complete each sentence.**

4. Pete's birthday was on 23rd _____ .

5. His aunt sent him a new _____.

6. Twelve of Pete's _____ and four of his
   _____ arrived for his party.

7. When is your birthday? Write a sentence to answer this
   question.

   _____

   _____

   _____

**Notes for teachers**
Read the story through with the children helping them to understand what has happened. Help them to compose a sentence to answer the final question, encouraging them to say the sentence out loud before writing it down.

## Pete's surprise

Name: _____

Date: _____

**Ring the correct answers.**

1. The word expensive means

   difficult to do        costing a lot of money        very big

2. Who was Pete's best friend?

   Jim          Jill          John          Josh

**Complete the sentences to answer the questions.**

3. Pete's aunt bought him a _____ for his birthday.

4. In the Africa part of the jigsaw there were pieces shaped like
   _____ and _____.

**Write a complete sentence to answer each of the following questions.**

5. When did Pete's grandparents arrive?

   _____

   _____

6. What shape was the cake Gran had made?

   _____

   _____

7. How did Pete feel at the end of the day?

   _____

   _____

**Notes for teachers**
Read the passage through with the children checking that they understand the sequence of events in the story. How did Pete's mood change throughout the day? Can they think of words to describe his different feelings? Help them to compose full sentences to answer the final two questions, encouraging them to say the sentences out loud before writing anything down.

**19**

Andrew Brodie: Improving Comprehension for ages 7-8 © A&C Black Publishers Ltd 2008

## Pete's surprise

Name: _____

Date: _____

1. Ring the word nearest in meaning to 'fascinating'.

   difficult        interesting        boring        unusual

**Write complete sentences to answer the following questions.**

2. Explain what the line 'it slowly dawned on Pete' means.

   _____

   _____

3. Who made Pete's birthday cake?

   _____

   _____

4. How many people were at Pete's birthday party altogether?

   _____

   _____

5. When Pete invited Josh to tea on his birthday, what did Josh tell him?

   _____

   _____

6. Explain why Josh's answer was an honest one.

   _____

   _____

**Notes for teachers**

Read the passage through with the children seeing if they can explain to you the main events in the story and how Pete felt at various points in the day. The answer to the final question should show that Josh was honest because he said he had 'plans to go out' and he actually was going out. He was going to Pete's party!

Andrew Brodie: Improving Comprehension for ages 7-8 © A&C Black Publishers Ltd 2008

# Max and the horse

"Climb on to my back," said the horse.

Max looked around to see if he could find a way to get up. There was a low wall that he could scramble on to and this sloped up to a higher section. He led the horse to the wall but struggled to climb it. He felt the horse's nose pushing him from behind and, with help, he was able to get on to the lower part and from there to the higher part of the wall.

The horse came alongside the wall. Max reached out and tried to pull himself on to the horse.

"Hold on to my mane," said the horse.

"Won't it hurt?" asked Max.

"Nothing hurts me," said the horse.

Max gripped the mane but, despite what the horse said, he held it as gently as he could.

"Hold tighter," said the horse, "you are going to need to pull."

"OK," said Max. He wound the hair of the mane between his fingers and pulled himself on to the horse's back, close to the horse's strong neck.

"Are you ready?" asked the horse.

"For what?" asked Max in reply.

"For this!" said the horse, and he began to trot, then to canter, then to gallop, then to fly!

Max gasped and clung tighter than ever.

Then he realised he had his eyes closed. As he opened them slowly, he couldn't believe what he saw...

Andrew Brodie: Improving Comprehension for ages 7-8 © A&C Black Publishers Ltd 2008

## Max and the horse

Name: _____

Date: _____

**Write a full sentence for each answer.**

1. What was the name of the boy in the story?

   _____

   _____

2. What did the horse ask the boy to do?

   _____

   _____

3. How did the horse help the boy to climb on?

   _____

   _____

4. What did the boy hold on to?

   _____

   _____

5. Where did the boy sit?

   _____

   _____

6. Describe how the horse was moving.

   _____

   _____

   _____

Andrew Brodie: Improving Comprehension for ages 7-8 © A&C Black Publishers Ltd 2008

## Max and the horse

Name: _____

Date: _____

### Answer the questions using full sentences.

1. How did Max get high enough to reach the horse's back?

_____

_____

2. What did the horse ask Max to hold on to?

_____

_____

3. Why did the horse ask Max to hold his mane tighter?

_____

_____

4. How did Max get a tight grip on the mane?

_____

_____

5. Describe how the horse was moving.

_____

_____

_____

6. Describe what it would feel like to fly on a horse.

_____

_____

**Notes for teachers**
Read the story through with the children helping them to visualise how Max managed to climb on to the horse. How does the author show how difficult it was? Discuss the ending of the story with them and what they think it would feel like to fly before answering the final question. They may need extra paper.

23

## Max and the horse

Name: _____

Date: _____

### Answer the questions using full sentences.

1. What was the wall like and how did this help Max?

_____

_____

2. Why didn't Max want to hold on to the mane at first?

_____

_____

3. Why did Max hold the mane gently?

_____

_____

4. Why did Max gasp at the end of the story?

_____

_____

5. What do you think happened next? Make up some more of the story.

_____

_____

_____

_____

_____

### Notes for teachers

Read the passage through with the children and help them match the questions to the appropriate part of the text to find the answers. The final question requires the children to think creatively. Encourage them to imagine that they are Max riding on a horse that is moving very fast through the air. What does it feel like? What can they see? Why do you think Max is leaving? Where do you think he is going?

# The history of the teddy bear

Teddy bears first became popular over a hundred years ago. In 1902 there was a story about an American president who refused to hurt a real bear when he was out hunting. That president was called Theodore Roosevelt. As Theodore was such a long name, his friends just called him Teddy. So because of the story about Teddy and the real bear, stuffed toy bears began to be called 'teddy bears'.

The first teddy bears were popular in the city of New York in America. At first teddy bears were a 'craze'. It wasn't just children who wanted to have bears, ladies were also seen carrying their teddies about and would even have their photographs taken with them!

Over the years, some teddy bears have become very famous. Winnie the Pooh, Rupert the Bear and Paddington Bear are perhaps the most well known of these famous bears.

Today, most babies or young children have at least one teddy. Many adults still have the teddy that they loved when they were children.

For more than seventy years children have been enjoying the song *Teddy Bears' Picnic*. Here are the some of the words.

*If you go down to the woods today*
*You're sure of a big surprise.*
*If you go down to the woods today*
*You'd better go in disguise.*
*For every bear that ever there was*
*Will gather there for certain, because*
*Today's the day the teddy bears have their picnic.*
*Every teddy bear who's been good*
*Is sure of a treat today.*
*There's lots of marvellous things to eat*
*And wonderful games to play.*
*Beneath the trees where nobody sees*
*They'll hide and seek as long as they please.*
*That's the way the teddy bears have their picnic.*

**Did you know?**

A group of teddies is called 'A hug of bears'.

Andrew Brodie: Improving Comprehension for ages 7-8 © A&C Black Publishers Ltd 2008

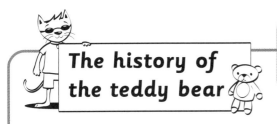

**The history of the teddy bear**

Name: _____

Date: _____

**Ring the correct answers.**

1. The first teddy bears were seen in which city?

   York          America          New York          Theodore

2. What is a group of teddies called?

   A hug of          A hug of          A kiss of          A kiss of
   teddies            bears             teddies            bears

3. What's the song about bears called?

   Teddy Bears'      Teddy Bears'      Teddy Bears'      Teddy Bears'
   Picnic            Party             Pudding           Pancake

**Fill in the missing words in the sentences below.**

4. The name of the president was _____

   _____.

5. His friends called him _____.

6. The teddy bears have their picnic in the _____.

**On a separate sheet of paper, draw a picture of your teddy bear. Write an interesting sentence about your picture.**

**Notes for teachers**
Read the passage through with the children helping them to understand the non-fiction text. If possible, as well as reading the words to 'Teddy Bears' Picnic', it would be helpful to play the children a recording of the song. Talk about their teddy bear with them so they can compose sentences orally before they write anything down.

## The history of the teddy bear

Name: _____

Date: _____

**Ring the correct answers.**

1. When did teddy bears first become popular?

   nearly one hundred years ago

   over one hundred years ago

   over seventy years ago

   exactly one hundred years ago

2. What did the American president refuse to do?

   | plant a | hurt a | take a | have a |
   | tree | real bear | photograph | picnic |

**Answer the next questions by writing complete sentences.**

3. What game are we told that teddy bears play when they are in the woods?

   _____

   _____

4. Who had their photographs taken with their teddies?

   _____

   _____

5. Can you name three famous bears?

   _____

   _____

**Notes for teachers**
Read the passage through with the children helping them to understand that it is a non-fiction text that conveys information. If possible, as well as reading the words to 'Teddy Bears' Picnic', it would be helpful to play the children a recording of the song. You could talk about their favourite cuddly toy – it might not be a teddy bear!

27

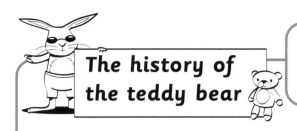

## The history of the teddy bear

Name: _____

Date: _____

1. Ring the word nearest in meaning to 'craze'.

   fun        fur        fringe        fashion

**Write complete sentences to answer the following questions.**

2. When teddies were first popular in America what are we told ladies would do with them?

   _____

   _____

3. Who was called 'Teddy', by his friends and why?

   _____

   _____

4. What do many adults still have?

   _____

   _____

5. Where might you get a big surprise?

   _____

   _____

**Do you have your own favourite soft toy. On a separate sheet of paper write a description of it and why it's important to you.**

**Notes for teachers**
Read the passage through with the children helping them to understand that it is a non-fiction text that conveys information. Talk about the use of different features on the page to show the different types of information. The answer to question 2 should mention that ladies carried their teddies about and had their photographs taken with them.

28

# Blackbirds

Blackbirds can be found all over our country. They are very common because they are happy to live in towns or in the country. Some blackbirds live in woods; some live in fields; some live in hilly areas; some live in flat areas; some live in gardens and others live in school grounds. If you look out of the window you might even see one now!

One of the strange things about blackbirds is that not all of them are black! The male blackbird is black with a yellow bill but the female blackbird is brown.

Blackbirds sing beautiful songs but they also make very loud sounds when they are frightened.

In the springtime, female blackbirds build nests made of dead leaves, dry grass, twigs and mud. Blackbirds are very good at building nests and the finished nests are very neat. The nests are hidden in trees or hedges.

A female blackbird will lay three, four or five eggs in the nest that she has made. The eggs are pale blue with brown spots and they are about three centimetres long. The female blackbird sits on her eggs to keep them warm. After about two weeks, the baby chicks peck their way out of the eggs. Both adult birds find food for the babies. The babies are always hungry and keep their parents very busy.

Andrew Brodie: Improving Comprehension for ages 7-8 © A&C Black Publishers Ltd 2008

## Blackbirds

### Write a full sentence for each answer.

1. What colour are male blackbirds?

   _____

   _____

2. What colour are female blackbirds?

   _____

   _____

3. What materials do blackbirds use to build their nests?

   _____

   _____

4. How many eggs does a female blackbird lay?

   _____

   _____

5. How does the blackbird keep her eggs warm?

   _____

   _____

6. What birds can you see today?

   _____

   _____

   _____

**Notes for teachers**
Read the passage through to the children helping them to understand that it is a non-fiction text and that a non-fiction text conveys information. If you feel that they are able to do so, help them to read it themselves using their phonic skills to decode any unfamiliar words.

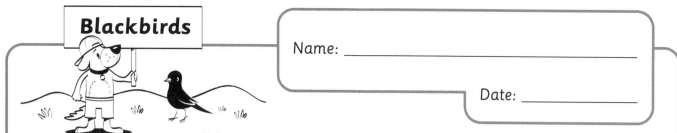

## Blackbirds

Name: _____

Date: _____

## Answer the questions using full sentences.

1. Name two of the places where blackbirds live.

   _____

   _____

2. Where could you find blackbirds' nests?

   _____

   _____

3. What colour are blackbirds' eggs?

   _____

   _____

4. Which of the parents keeps the eggs warm?

   _____

   _____

5. How do the blackbird chicks get out of the eggs?

   _____

   _____

6. If you saw a blackbird how could you tell if it was male or female?

   _____

   _____

   _____

**Notes for teachers**

Read the passage through with the children helping them to understand the non-fiction text and what features make it non-fiction. Can they identify and talk about the main points of the text?

Andrew Brodie: Improving Comprehension for ages 7-8 © A&C Black Publishers Ltd 2008

## Blackbirds

Name: _____

Date: _____

### Answer the questions using full sentences.

1. Why are blackbirds common in this country?

   _____

   _____

2. Describe some of the ways in which the female blackbird is different from the male blackbird.

   _____

   _____

   _____

3. Why might it be difficult to find blackbirds' nests?

   _____

   _____

   _____

4. How might you be able to tell if you were right if you think you saw a blackbird?

   _____

   _____

**Choose a bird that you can describe. You can use the library or a computer to find your information. Write about the bird you have chosen on a separate sheet of paper.**

**Notes for teachers**
Read the non-fiction text with the children, talking about the features that make it different from a story. The questions may be answered with simple sentences but there is enough information in the text to provide longer answers e.g. question 2 could be answered simply in relation to the birds' appearance but the pupils may also be able to explain that the female builds the nest and keeps the eggs warm and the male does not.

# In the middle of the night

One cold night in winter Mr Brown woke up in the middle of the night. He looked at his clock: one fifteen it said. Mr Brown didn't know why he had woken up. Was there a noise? Yes, there it was again. Was it an aeroplane? It sounded like a jet engine.

Mr Brown climbed out of bed and put on his slippers. Whatever the noise was he didn't want cold feet! He could still hear the noise. It sounded like the roar of a dragon, or was it the snore of a dragon sleeping in Mr Brown's garden?

Mr Brown opened the window and leaned out, but not too far because he didn't want to fall out. The noise was still there.

He went downstairs and unlocked the back door. He stepped out into the cold. The moon was shining brightly, so brightly that it was almost like daylight.

Although Mr Brown was a bit frightened he walked down the garden path. An owl hooted but that was not the only noise because the roaring, snoring jet engine sound was still there, going on and on.

At the end of the garden Mr Brown looked over the wall. There were lots of bright lights shining and then finally he saw what was making the noise. It was a great big machine on the railway line.

The machine was moving along very slowly. It had lots of bright lights. There were groups of men working around it. The machine was picking up the railway sleepers, stirring up all the stones, then putting the sleepers down again.

Mr Brown went back to bed. He was able to sleep again now he knew what was making the noise. It wasn't a dragon or a jet engine, but he was glad he checked as it very easily could have been!

Andrew Brodie: Improving Comprehension for ages 7-8 © A&C Black Publishers Ltd 2008

**In the middle of the night**

Name: _____

Date: _____

**Write a full sentence for each answer. Don't forget to start each sentence with a capital letter and to end it with a full stop.**

1. Who woke up in the middle of the night?

   _____

   _____

2. At first, what did Mr Brown think was making the noise?

   _____

   _____

3. What did he put on his feet?

   _____

   _____

4. Where did he go?

   _____

   _____

5. What did he discover was making the noise?

   _____

   _____

6. What did he do at the end of the story?

   _____

   _____

**Notes for teachers**
Discuss the passage with the children and check they understand what has happened in the story. Did they like the story? Did they understand why Mr Brown might have been scared? Remind them to use full stops and capital letters to punctuate their sentences.

34

Andrew Brodie: Improving Comprehension for ages 7-8 © A&C Black Publishers Ltd 2008

**In the middle
of the night**

Name: _____

Date: _____

## Answer the questions using full sentences.

1. Why did Mr Brown wake up?

   _____

   _____

2. At first Mr Brown thought a jet plane was making the noise.
   What other idea did he have?

   _____

   _____

3. What other sound did Mr Brown hear when he went outside?

   _____

   _____

4. What did he discover was making the noise?

   _____

   _____

5. Where was the railway line?

   _____

   _____

6. Why did Mr Brown feel able to sleep at the end of the story?

   _____

   _____

**Notes for teachers**
Read the passage with the children and discuss the storyline. How do they think Mr Brown felt when he heard the noise? Was he surprised when he found out what it was? If time allows, you could role-play the conversation the next day with Mr Brown telling a friend/neighbour about the episode.

Andrew Brodie: Improving Comprehension for ages 7-8 © A&C Black Publishers Ltd 2008

Name: _____

Date: _____

**Answer the questions using full sentences.**

1. At what time did Mr Brown wake up?

   _____

   _____

2. Why did Mr Brown put his slippers on?

   _____

   _____

3. Why was it so light outside even though it was the middle of the night?

   _____

   _____

4. Describe what Mr Brown saw when he looked over the garden wall.

   _____

   _____

   _____

   _____

   _____

**On a separate sheet of paper, describe a time when you were woken up in the middle of the night. What woke you up? Were you frightened? Were you able to get back to sleep quite quickly?**

**Notes for teachers**
Read the passage through with the children and then see if they can summarise the main events of the story. For question 4, they need to re-read the story carefully and then they should include the following features: the machine, the lights, the men, the railway line, the railway sleepers and the stones.

# Hans Christian Andersen

Hans Christian Andersen was born in Denmark in 1805. He lived with his parents in a town called Odense. They were a very poor family who couldn't afford to send Hans Christian to school.

As a little boy, Hans Christian enjoyed making up fairy tales and puppet shows. When he was only eleven years old, his father died and he had to go out to work to earn money to help his mother.

Three years later, when Hans Christian was fourteen years old, he left home and went to the city of Copenhagen to seek fame and fortune . He didn't do very well there to begin with but eventually he was able to go back to school and then on to university to continue his education.

He wrote fairy tales and stories for children and soon became famous. At first he wrote the stories that he had heard when he was a child and then began to make up new tales. During his seventy-one year life, Hans Christian Andersen wrote over three hundred stories.

Many of his stories are still enjoyed by children today. Among his best-known stories are: The Emperor's New Clothes, The Ugly duckling, The Snow Queen, The Princess and the Pea, and the Little Mermaid.

Andrew Brodie: Improving Comprehension for ages 7-8 © A&C Black Publishers Ltd 2008

## Hans Christian Andersen

Name: _____

Date: _____

**Ring the correct answers**

1.  Where was Hans Christian Andersen born?

    England        America        Denmark        France

2.  In what year was he born?

    1905        1906        1806        1805

3.  He wrote the story of 'The Little... '

    Mouse        Mermaid        Milkman        Monkey

**Fill in the missing words to complete the sentences.**

4.  As a boy Hans Christian made up _____ tales and _____ shows.

5.  He was _____ years old when he died.

6.  One of his most famous stories was 'The Ugly _____'.

**Write a sentence to answer this question.**

7.  How many stories did Hans Anderson write?

    _____

    _____

8.  Can you name three of Hans Anderson's stories?

    _____

    _____

    _____

**Notes for teachers**
Read the passage with the children and talk about the main events in the life of Hans Christian. Do they know what genre of text this is (a biography)? Have they heard of any Hans Christian Anderson stories? What did they like/dislike about the stories?

Andrew Brodie: Improving Comprehension for ages 7-8 © A&C Black Publishers Ltd 2008

**Hans Christian Andersen**

Name: _____

Date: _____

## Ring the correct answer.

1. Odense is the name of a town in

   Denmark      England      Spain      Scotland

2. Hans Christian Andersen's family were very

   happy      sad      rich      poor

## Complete the sentences to answer the questions.

3. How old was Hans Christian when his father died?
   Hans Christian was _____ years old when
   his _____ died.

4. How many stories did Hans Christian Andersen write?
   He wrote _____ stories.

## Write complete sentences to answer the questions below.

5. Why did Hans Christian go to work after his father died?

   _____

   _____

6. How did he become famous?

   _____

   _____

   _____

**Notes for teachers**
Read the passage with the children and see if they can remember the main events in the life of Hans Christian.
Do they know what genre of text this is (a biography)? Do they know of any other biographies? Have they ever
tried to write a biography of someone?

Andrew Brodie: Improving Comprehension for ages 7-8 © A&C Black Publishers Ltd 2008

1.  Ring the word nearest in meaning to 'author'.

    dancer          writer          artist          teacher

2.  Which of the following is nearest in meaning to 'fame and fortune'?

    to be well-known and rich

    to work very hard to earn some money

    to be on a television show

    to be poor and tired

**Write complete sentences to answer these questions.**

3.  How old was Hans Christian when he left home?

    _____

    _____

4.  Where did he go to seek fame and fortune?

    _____

    _____

5.  What sort of stories were the first ones he wrote?

    _____

    _____

    _____

**Notes for teachers**
Read the passage through with the children helping them to spot the significant events in Hans Christian's life. For question 2 you could suggest to the children that they substitute each of the four alternative answers for the words 'fame and fortune' in the appropriate sentence in the text to help them to identify which one is correct.

**40**

# The Emperor's new clothes (Part 1)

Long ago in a far away land there was an Emperor who loved clothes. Each day he would look in his enormous wardrobe to decide what to wear. The Emperor liked to wear something different every day and hoped to be the best-dressed man wherever he went.

When new fashions came out he was the first to try them. Sometimes these new fads suited him and sometimes they didn't!

One day, two strangers arrived at the Emperor's palace. They told the Emperor that they were weavers and that they wove the finest cloth in the world.

"Our thread is magical," said one of the strangers.

"The cloth we make from our thread can only be seen by very clever people," explained the other.

"It's invisible to stupid people," added the first stranger.

"Which makes it very expensive," said the second one.

"I don't care about the price," said the Emperor excitedly. "I simply must have a suit made from this cloth!"

The strangers agreed to make the new suit at the palace and set up looms to weave the thread into cloth. The Emperor paid the strangers a huge amount of money to make his new clothes. He was too excited to consider the possibility that perhaps this magical thread was too good to be true.

Unfortunately the strangers were not honest men. They had no thread and were not making magic cloth on their loom. They were cheats who hoped to take a lot of money from the Emperor and give him nothing in return. Once they had set up their looms, they told the Emperor they needed to be left alone until the suit was ready for the Emperor to try on.

The Emperor told everyone in the land about the wonderful new suit he was having made and announced that there would be a parade so that they would all be able to see him wearing it. He thought that he would soon find out which of the people in his land were clever people and which were not.

Andrew Brodie: Improving Comprehension for ages 7-8 © A&C Black Publishers Ltd 2008

## The Emperor's new clothes (Part 1)

Name: _____

Date: _____

**Ring the correct answers.**

1. What is the title of the story?

   The King's clothes

   The Emperor's new clothes

   The Emperor's clothes

   The King's new clothes

2. What did the Emperor love?

   football        weaving        palaces        clothes

3. How many strangers arrived to see the Emperor?

   one        two        three        four

**Fill in the missing words to complete the sentences.**

4. Where did the strangers agree to make the new suit?
   The strangers said they would make the suit at the _____

   _____ .

5. What were the strangers really going to give the Emperor?

   The strangers were going to give the Emperor _____

   _____ .

**On a separate sheet draw a picture of yourself in your favourite clothes. Write an interesting sentence about your picture.**

Andrew Brodie: Improving Comprehension for ages 7-8 © A&C Black Publishers Ltd 2008

## The Emperor's new clothes (Part 1)

Name: _____

Date: _____

**Ring the correct answers.**

1. Which of the words below best describes the strangers?

   weavers          honest          cheats          magical

2. Who did they say were the only people that would be able to see the cloth?

   clever          kind          brave          silly

   people          people          people          people

**Complete the sentences.**

3. _____ liked to be the first to try new fashions.

4. The strangers hoped to take_____from the Emperor.

**Write complete sentences to answer the questions.**

5. After setting up their looms, what did the strangers say they needed?

   _____

   _____

6. Why was the Emperor going to organise a parade?

   _____

   _____

**Notes for teachers**
This is a very challenging text and some children are likely to need a lot of help in reading and understanding it. In answering question 5, pupils should indicate that the strangers asked for peace and quiet. For question 6, pupils should say that the Emperor was organising a parade to ensure that everyone in the land saw his new clothes.

Andrew Brodie: Improving Comprehension for ages 7-8 © A&C Black Publishers Ltd 2008

| The Emperor's new clothes (Part 1) | Name: _____ |
| --- | --- |
| | Date: _____ |

1.  Which words are nearest in meaning to 'fad'?

    popular for a          completely          smart          clothes that
      short while           ridiculous          clothes         were new

**Answer the following questions with whole sentences.**

2.  What did the cheats say was special about their cloth?

    _____

    _____

3.  Why do you think the strangers really wanted to be left
    alone until the suit was ready to be tried on?

    _____

    _____

4.  Do you think the Emperor thought he would be able to see
    the suit? Explain your answer.

    _____

    _____

    _____

5.  What did the Emperor think he would find out when other
    people saw him in his new clothes?

    _____

    _____

**Notes for teachers**
Read the passage through with the children and discuss the sequence of events in the story. Do they think this story is complete? If not, why not? In the final question pupils should realise that the Emperor clearly assumed he was clever enough to see the cloth as otherwise he would not have wished to parade through the streets in his new suit. Any other reasonable explanation can also be accepted.

44

# The Emperor's new clothes (Part 2)

After six weeks the strangers, who were now known as the royal weavers, announced that the wonderful new suit was ready for the Emperor to try on.

The Emperor went to see his new suit. The weavers pretended to hold up the most magnificent suit when actually they were holding nothing at all. They described the many colours of the cloth, the style of the suit and the marvellous buttons it had.

To his amazement the Emperor, of course, didn't see anything as there was nothing to see. He was alarmed as he thought that this must mean he was rather stupid. So he said that it was the most marvellous suit he had ever seen.

The day of the great parade arrived. The Emperor once again allowed the weavers to dress him in this imaginary suit, all the time wishing he could really see it. He walked through the great rooms of the palace where to the courtiers it looked as if he was wearing only his woolly underwear. None of them dared to say anything in case they were thought too stupid to keep their jobs. Instead, they admired the suit's wonderful colours, the marvellous buttons and the excellent way the suit fitted the Emperor.

The parade started and the people cheered as the Emperor came into view. They were all worried when all they could see was the Emperor in his underwear so they just pretended they could see the suit. After about an hour, a little boy in the crowd started to laugh and asked his parents why the Emperor had forgotten to put on his clothes. Soon more of the crowd began to laugh and eventually everyone realised that the Emperor had no clothes on.

The most amazing colour worn by the Emperor that day was the scarlet of his cheeks as they burned with the knowledge that he was indeed rather stupid. His foolishness and vanity had led him to pay a vast fortune to wear clothes made of nothing!

Just in case you are wondering what happened to the cheating weavers, they left the land, with all their takings, as the parade started and were never seen again.

Andrew Brodie: Improving Comprehension for ages 7-8 © A&C Black Publishers Ltd 2008

## The Emperor's new clothes (Part 2)

Name: _____

Date: _____

**Ring the correct answers.**

1. How long was it before the weavers said the suit was ready for the Emperor to see?

   six days        six weeks        six months        six years

2. Which word is used to describe the buttons on the suit?

   magnificent        colourful        marvellous        amazing

3. Who was the first person to laugh when he saw the Emperor?

   a little girl        a little boy        a lady        a man

**Fill in the missing words.**

4. On the day of the parade the _____ dressed the Emperor.

5. The people _____ as the Emperor came into view.

**Answer the next question with a full sentence.**

6. What happened to the cheating weavers?

   _____

   _____

   _____

**Notes for teachers**
Remind the children of what happened in Part 1 before reading this passage. Read the passage together and then discuss the major events. Do they understand what has happened? What sort of person is the Emperor? What sort of people are the weavers?

## The Emperor's new clothes (Part 2)

Name: _____

Date: _____

**Ring the correct answers**

1. What did the Emperor wear at the parade?

   underwear          new suit          swimwear          coat

2. Who felt rather stupid after the parade?

   the                the                the                the
   little boy         weavers            courtiers          Emperor

**Complete the sentences.**

3. The courtiers were afraid that if they admitted they couldn't

   see the suit they would _____

   _____.

4. The crowds realised that the Emperor _____

   _____ .

**Answer the questions with complete sentences.**

5. Why was the Emperor surprised when he went to see his new suit?

   _____

   _____

6. How much are we told he paid for his suit of nothing at all?

   _____

   _____

**47**

## The Emperor's new clothes (Part 2)

Name: _____

Date: _____

1.  Ring the word nearest in meaning to 'scarlet'.

    hot          colour          red          scared

**Write complete sentences to answer the questions.**

2.  What did the Emperor wear on the day of the parade?

    _____

    _____

3.  Why didn't the Emperor say he couldn't see his new suit?

    _____

    _____

4.  What made the Emperor realise that he had been stupid?

    _____

    _____

5.  Why didn't the weavers stay to watch the parade?

    _____

    _____

6.  What do you think the Emperor might have done after returning to his palace?

    _____

    _____

    _____

**Notes for teachers**
Discuss the events of Part 1 before reading the passage through with the children helping them to follow the story. Before tackling the final question pupils should be encouraged to discuss their ideas. Help them to realise that the answer to this question can't be found in the text. Any reasonable idea written in a well-constructed sentence (or sentences) should be accepted.

# A letter from the weavers

*When the cheating weavers arrived at the palace they had brought
with them a letter of introduction asking the Emperor to see them.
This is what they wrote:*

Your Most Royal Wonderfulness,

We have heard that you are the most smartly dressed man in the whole of
this lovely country. We thought you might be interested in knowing
about the wonderful suits we can weave from a thread that has never
before been seen in this country.

This thread has been obtained, at considerable danger to ourselves, from
plants in the valleys of the enchanted woodlands many hundreds of miles
away. It has some of the most brilliant colours imaginable. There are vivid
emerald greens, rubies, lemon yellows and the most stunning sapphire
blues.

The most exciting feature of the thread is that it will help the owner to
find out how clever or foolish their friends, neighbours and servants are.
This is because only clever people can see the amazing cloth that we have
woven from the thread.

As you might imagine we are kept very busy making suits for the
wealthiest and most important people in the countries we visit. We limit
our work to only one new suit in each country.

We would like you to be the first person to look at our thread. If you can
see us today we might well be able to do business with you.
Unfortunately, we can't wait until tomorrow as we are in such high
demand.

Highest regards,

Fraud and Felon  (Master weavers)

## A letter from the weavers

Name: _____

Date: _____

**Ring the correct answers.**

1. Who did the weavers want to see?

   the King        the Queen        the Emperor        the Prince

2. How many weavers did the letter come from?

   one        two        three        four

3. Who, did they say, could see the cloth?

   foolish        clever        thoughtless        tall
   people         people         people            people

**Write the correct words to complete the sentences.**

4. The letter begins with the words, 'Your Most _____
   _____ '.

5. The letter says that the weavers had heard the Emperor was
   the most _____ dressed man in the country.

**Write a sentence to answer this question.**

6. What do you think of the weavers?

   _____

   _____

   _____

   _____

**Notes for teachers**
Read the letter through with the children. This is a very challenging text and the children are likely to need a lot of help in reading and understanding it. The final question requires the children to think about the whole story of the Emperor's New Clothes, making their own judgement about the behaviour of the weavers. Help the children to compose a sentence, encouraging them to say the sentence out loud before writing it down.

Andrew Brodie: Improving Comprehension for ages 7-8 © A&C Black Publishers Ltd 2008

## A letter from the weavers

Name: _____

Date: _____

### Ring the correct answers.

1. Sapphire is a word used to describe a shade of

   red          yellow          green          blue

2. When did the weavers say they wanted to see the Emperor?

   today          tomorrow          next week          this week

### Complete the sentences.

3. The weavers said that the thread was found in the
   _____ woodlands.

4. They said they could not wait because they were
   in such _____.

### Write complete sentences to answer the next questions.

5. Who do the weavers say they make suits for?

   _____

   _____

6. How far away was the place where the weavers said they
   found the magical thread?

   _____

   _____

   _____

**Notes for teachers**
Read the letter with the children and point out the features that make it a letter. Why do they think the weavers introduced themselves using a letter? How did the weavers persuade the Emperor to see them?

51

## A letter from the weavers

Name: _____

Date: _____

1. Ring the words nearest in meaning to 'fraud and felon'.

   fool and idiot          weaver and tailor          cheat and criminal          teacher and artist

**Write complete sentences to answer these questions.**

2. Why do you think the letter started by addressing the Emperor as 'Your most royal wonderfulness'?

   _____

   _____

3. List three adjectives used in the second paragraph to describe the brightness of the colours.

   _____

   _____

   _____

4. Why do you think the weavers only made one suit in each country?

   _____

   _____

5. How far away did the weavers say they had to go to find the thread?

   _____

   _____

**Notes for teachers**
Read the introduction and the letter through with the children. The answer to question 2 should indicate the weavers attempt to flatter the Emperor. The adjectives listed in question three should be 'vivid', 'brilliant' and 'stunning'. The answer to question 4 should indicate that after making one suit the weavers would need to leave as their dishonesty would have been discovered.

# A day out

It was Saturday morning. Gita and Adit got up early.

"Are you two ready?" asked Mum.

Mum and Dad were up and dressed already and had been very busy getting everything ready. There was a big pile of things by the front door. Gita was desperate for breakfast but Dad said they would stop on the way for something to eat.

They put the things in the car and off they went. After an hour, they stopped for breakfast at a motorway service station.  Gita and Adit both had toast then an apple. They had orange juice to drink. Mum and Dad had coffee.

After half an hour they set off again. An hour later, they arrived. Gita and Adit rushed out of the car.

"I love the sea," said Adit.

"I love the sand," said Gita.

The two children raced towards the steps that led down to the sand.

"Wait!" called Mum. "It's dangerous to run off. There are lots of people about and you might get lost. Just wait for us. In fact, you can carry some of these things because most of them are yours!"

Gita and Adit helped unload the boot. There were lots of things to carry: buckets, spades, towels, a picnic box, a bag of drinks, picnic blankets, a wind-break with a mallet for hammering it into the sand, a cricket bat with a ball and a large football. The two children couldn't move so quickly now as they had too much to carry.

The family walked carefully down the steps and reached the sand. They looked for a big patch of sand where they could put up their wind-break and spread out their blankets but everywhere was busy.

"Look, there's a spot near the ice-cream van!" said Gita.

"All right," said Dad. "That's a good spot."

Andrew Brodie: Improving Comprehension for ages 7-8 © A&C Black Publishers Ltd 2008

## A day out

Name: _____

Date: _____

**Answer the questions using full sentences.**

1. Who got up first? Was it Gita and Adit or was it Mum and Dad?

   _____

   _____

2. Who was desperate for breakfast?

   _____

   _____

3. What did Gita and Adit have to eat?

   _____

   _____

4. Where were the two children racing to get to?

   _____

   _____

5. Where did they decide to sit?

   _____

   _____

6. Where do you love to go?

   _____

   _____

   _____

**Notes for teachers**

Read the passage through to the children helping them to understand what has happened in the text. Note that the word 'beach' does not appear and it would be useful to discuss with the children the location of the family at the end of the story. Discuss the final question with the children. Ideas could include the beach, the countryside, the shopping centre, a particular shop, a football ground, a park.

Andrew Brodie: Improving Comprehension for ages 7-8 © A&C Black Publishers Ltd 2008

## A day out

Name: _____

Date: _____

**Answer the questions using full sentences.**

1 Why did Mum and Dad get up early?

_____

_____

2. Where did the family have breakfast?

_____

_____

3. What did they all have to drink?

_____

_____

4. Where did the family arrive at the end of their journey?

_____

_____

5. What did the children do as soon as they arrived?

_____

_____

**On a separate piece of paper describe a special day out that you have enjoyed. How long did it take to get there? Who went on this trip? What did you take with you? What was the place you visited like?**

**Notes for teachers**
Read the passage through to the children helping them to understand the sequence of events. Note that the word 'beach' does not appear so it would be useful to discuss with the children where they think the family has arrived at the end of the story. Discuss the final question with the children – this is their chance to write about an actual experience but it can be difficult for some children to remember things they have done or places they have been to so you could suggest the beach, the countryside, the shopping centre, a particular shop, a football ground, a park, the zoo, etc.

## A day out

**Answer the questions using full sentences.**

1. Why did Dad say Gita couldn't have breakfast?

   _____

   _____

2. How long after leaving home did they stop for breakfast?

   _____

   _____

3. For how long did they stop at the motorway services?

   _____

   _____

4. Why did Mum tell the children to wait?

   _____

   _____

5. Where did the family decide to put up their windbreak and spread out their blankets?

   _____

   _____

**On a separate piece of paper describe a day out you have had. What made it special?**

# Building a sandcastle

Mum and Dad were reading the newspaper. Gita was reading her magazine. Adit was bored. He decided to build a sandcastle.

Adit scooped sand into the bigger of the two buckets until the bucket was full to the top then he smoothed out the sand. He tipped the bucket over carefully, patted the base of it with his spade then lifted the bucket slowly. Brilliant, he thought, as he looked at his perfect tower of sand.

He filled the bucket again and tipped the second bucketful of sand right next to the first one. Then he did it again and again, tipping the sand very carefully so that each new tower was just touching the others that were already there.

Adit now had four towers arranged in a square. The sand was perfect – not too dry and not too wet – so it stuck together well.

Adit decided to fill the hole in the middle of the four towers. He scooped up some sand in the smaller bucket then tried to pour it slowly into the gap but it fell out of the bucket in clumps and knocked the edges off the inner parts of his towers.

Adit was not pleased. He wondered whether to knock all the towers down. He nearly did but then decided that he could still fill the hole between the towers if he was really careful.

He used the spade this time, instead of the bucket, and poured small amounts of sand into the gap. He kept putting more in until his new pile of sand in the middle of the towers was taller than the towers themselves. Then he used the spade to flatten it out so that he had a big square castle.

Now he was able to make a new tower on top of the square that he had already. He found some small stones and shells and pressed them into the sand to make windows. It looked great.

"Look at my sandcastle," said Adit proudly.

He looked round at the others but all three of them had fallen asleep in the sunshine.

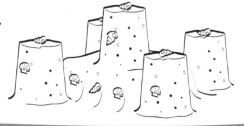

Andrew Brodie: Improving Comprehension for ages 7-8 © A&C Black Publishers Ltd 2008

## Building a sandcastle

Name: _____

Date: _____

**Answer the questions using full sentences.**

1.  What were Mum, Dad and Gita all doing?

    _____

    _____

2.  What did Adit decide to do?

    _____

    _____

3.  How many buckets did Adit have?

    _____

    _____

4.  Which bucket did Adit use to build his towers?

    _____

    _____

5.  What did Adit use to fill the hole between the towers?

    _____

    _____

6.  Why didn't Mum, Dad and Gita see Adit's sandcastle?

    _____

    _____

    _____

**Notes for teachers**
Read the passage through to the children discussing what has happened in the story and how Adit might be feeling at various points. Help the children to compose answers to the questions orally before they write anything down. Encourage them to use full stops at the ends of their sentences and to use capital letters for the starts of sentences and for the initial letters of people's names.

Andrew Brodie: Improving Comprehension for ages 7-8 © A&C Black Publishers Ltd 2008

## Building a sandcastle

Name: _____

Date: _____

**Answer the questions using full sentences.**

1. Why did Adit decide to build a sandcastle?

   _____

   _____

2. What did Adit think of his first tower?

   _____

   _____

3. Why was the sand so good for the job?

   _____

   _____

4. What was Adit not pleased about?

   _____

   _____

5. What was the last thing Adit did to his sandcastle?

   _____

   _____

6. Have you ever made a sandcastle?

   _____

   _____

   _____

**Notes for teachers**
Read the passage through with the children seeing if they can remember the main events of the story. The final question could simply be answered with 'yes' or 'no' but remind the pupils that they are practising writing sentences and encourage them to provide more detail.

**59**

## Building a sandcastle

Name: _____

Date: _____

**Write some instructions for building a sandcastle. Number your instructions. Make sure each instruction is a full sentence. Use the story to find some clues.**

_____

_____

_____

_____

_____

_____

_____

_____

_____

_____

_____

_____

_____

_____

_____

_____

**Notes for teachers**
Discuss the task on this worksheet with the children and encourage them to notice that they could follow the same procedure as Adit, in order to create a set of numbered instructions. Ensure that they use capital letters and full stops appropriately and that they write using handwriting in accordance with the school's handwriting policy.

Andrew Brodie: Improving Comprehension for ages 7-8 © A&C Black Publishers Ltd 2008

# Fetching the water

Gita woke up. She was hot. She had lots of sun cream on so she wouldn't get burnt but she still felt too hot.

She sat up and rubbed her eyes. Adit had made a really good sandcastle.

"I like your sandcastle, Adit," she said.

"Thanks," said Adit.

"It needs a moat," said Gita.

"What's a moat?" asked Adit.

"Real castles sometimes have moats," said Gita. "It's like a big wide ditch full of water all the way round the castle."

"That would be good," said Adit.

"You dig the ditch and I'll get some water," said Gita. She jumped up and picked up the two buckets. "See you in a minute," she said, and started running down the beach.

The beach was really crowded but Gita knew she could find Mum, Dad and Dan again because their patch was right next to the ice cream van.

It took ages to get to the sea because the tide was out. When she got there she filled the two buckets then paddled in the water. It was lovely and she was so hot that she decided to sit down in it. Then she jumped up and splashed with her feet as much as she could. It was great.

Suddenly she remembered that Adit needed the water for his moat. She filled the buckets again because some of the water had tipped out. Then she started walking up the beach.

She couldn't see Mum, Dad and Adit. She could see an ice cream van but there was another one … and another. Which was the right one?

"Gita," called Mum. "Where have you been?"

What a relief! Mum had come down the beach to find her.

Andrew Brodie: Improving Comprehension for ages 7-8 © A&C Black Publishers Ltd 2008

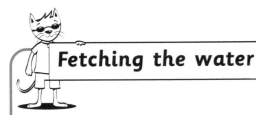

Name: _____

Date: _____

**Answer the questions using full sentences.**

1.  What is the name of the girl in this story?

    _____

    _____

2.  How did the girl feel at the start of the story?

    _____

    _____

3.  What is the name of the girl's brother?

    _____

    _____

4.  What had her brother made?

    _____

    _____

5.  What did the girl go to fetch?

    _____

    _____

6.  How many ice cream vans could the girl see?

    _____

    _____

**Notes for teachers**

Read the passage through to the children helping them to understand the story. Help them to compose sentences to answer the questions, encouraging them to say the sentences out loud before writing them down e.g. for question 1 some children might write: 'The name of the girl was called Gita.' Saying it out loud will help them to realize that a more appropriate answer would be either of the following: 'The name of the girl was Gita.' or 'The girl was called Gita.' Use the opportunity to explain that children should be very careful not to get lost on the beach or anywhere else. Gita should have told her parents that she was going to collect the water and should perhaps have taken Adit with her.

Andrew Brodie: Improving Comprehension for ages 7-8 © A&C Black Publishers Ltd 2008

## Fetching the water

Name: _____

Date: _____

**Answer the questions using full sentences.**

1. What did Gita think of Adit's sandcastle?

   _____

   _____

2. What did Gita say the sandcastle needed?

   _____

   _____

3. Why did Gita think she would be able to find her family easily?

   _____

   _____

4. Why did it take a long time to reach the water?

   _____

   _____

5. What did Gita do when she reached the sea?

   _____

   _____

6. Why wasn't it easy for Gita to find her family?

   _____

   _____

**Notes for teachers**

Read the passage through with the children helping them to understand the story. Help them to compose sentences to answer the questions, encouraging them to say the sentences out loud before writing them down. Use the opportunity to explain that children should be very careful not to get lost on the beach or anywhere else. Gita should have told her parents that she was going to collect the water and should perhaps have taken Adit with her.

Andrew Brodie: Improving Comprehension for ages 7-8 © A&C Black Publishers Ltd 2008

## Fetching the water

**Answer the questions using full sentences.**

1.  What had Gita been doing before she saw Adit's sandcastle?

    _____

    _____

2.  Why didn't Gita get burnt?

    _____

    _____

3.  What is a moat? Describe it.

    _____

    _____

    _____

4.  Why did it take a long time to reach the sea?

    _____

    _____

5.  Why did Gita have to fill the buckets twice?

    _____

    _____

**On a separate sheet of paper, write about what you think happened next.**

**Notes for teachers**
Read the passage through with the children discussing what has happened in the previous story and helping them to remember the main events in this one. Before they complete the last question it would be a good idea to discuss what happened next with the children, encouraging them to think that Gita did get back to her family safely. Use the opportunity to explain that children should be very careful not to get lost on the beach or anywhere else. Gita should have told her parents that she was going to collect the water and should perhaps have taken Adit with her.